Divine Design:

A Prelude To Poetry Of The Future

-Part II: Spirit Vibe

By Alan Peter Garfoot

Divine Design: A Prelude To Poetry Of The Future-
Part II: Spirit Vibe

By Alan Peter Garfoot

© Alan Peter Garfoot 2022

© Cover Photo By 'T' Teigan J.R. Simmonite

ISBN: 978-1-4717-2432-9

© The New World Thought Disorder 2022

Lulu Press Imprint.

(2022)

London.

Contents

To my lifelong friend Rory Mayfield....

Absolute total legend....

Also Published By The New World Thought Disorder:

The Research Economy
Aspire To Inspire
The Infinity Theorem
Divine Design: Soul Nature
Divine Design: Mind Shine

<u>Figure It Out</u>

Emerge my friends,
As glorious beings,
Achieve your potential,
And realise your dreams.

Harmonise with me,
The elements of mind,
The soul within the self,
And its spiritual design.

Project your astral self,
To a far off world,
And find original meanings,
Constructed of new words.

Let us ascend the stars,
Through an inspirational love,
As we sail the cosmos,
In the heavens high above.

So ink with me a moment,
Where we can truly see,
The inner nature of beauty,
And true dynamics of reality.

Awakened Self

The essence,
Of your love,
Is a perfection,
Of the heart,
You inspire,
A gentle peace,
And subtle affection,
Of the empowerment,
Of a profound nature,
And inspired soul.
As we share,
A spiritual embrace,
The stars fall,
From the heavens,
And the enlightenment,
Of the cosmos,
Are at your feet,
A true master,
Of the nature,
And the totality,
Of the energies,
Of the awakened self,
And the enlightened soul.

Black Lives Matter

A nation of race hate,
Social equation that segregates,
Loses face, waits and then hesitates,
Teaching us oppression is our fate.

I hear the turmoil and the cries,
As the wool gets pulled over our eyes,
By an elitist state which so lies,
As it tries to disguise its social divides.

We need the Police brutality,
To cease to be a reality,
For only peace, love and equality,
Should ever be our ideology.

For we need political accountability,
To harness our individual liberty,
And create out of our possibility,
The miracle of our future positivity.

Energy Of Our Love

The sacred energy,
Of our love,
Is the greatest,
Empowerment,
Ive ever felt,
The essence,
Of your grace,
Is the purest,
Of perfections,
In the universe,
Every time,
Our spirits touch,
Our souls share,
The sweet embrace,
Of true love,
Our hearts,
Sharing the energy,
Of our affections,
And the beauty,
Of our immortal,
True desires,
So lay with me,
And resonate,
The vibrations,
Of our love.

Yeah For Sure

If we ever,
Get our shit together,
Our lives will get better,
In true love sealed forever.

As our essences are so refined,
We harmonise our energies of mind,
To the universes divine designs,
Of our aligned hearts that so shine.

The perfection of our affection,
Strengthens our soul connection,
Reflecting on our passions dimensions,
The loving creation of our fate's direction.

So with your heart so pure,
I adore you even more,
As the cure for my core,
I so love you forever more.

Vibrations Of Love

My sweetheart,
Life the effortlessness,
Of your grace,
And affection,
So too the flawlessness,
Of your beauty,
Is a p[perfection,
Of cosmic essence,
our inner nature,
Shines resplendent,
The creator in your aura,
Your spirit shines,
And sets your heart aflame,
Realise your desire,
True perspective again,
And real self,
In your dreams,
And become whole,
Your highest virtues,
Of the soul.

Unification Of Duality

Through the focus,
Of our subtle will,
Into the manifestation,
Of our dreams and desires,
Through the intentionality,
Of the subconscious mind,
The dynamics of the dispositions,
Refined into a harmony,
Of our essence within ourselves,
Our innermost unifying seal,
Of the sacred core,
The divine connection,
Between self and soul,
Through the essence,
Of the many colours,
Of our complex nature,
Through the pursuit,
Of the perfection,
Of the dynamics of the will,
For its empathic truth,
The resonance of our duality,
Into a singularity of love.

Definitions Of Destiny

The energy inside,
Of an inspired dynamic,
The resolute will,
To save the planet.

Essences which shine,
Of an inspired soul,
The true comprehension,
Of the unified whole.

The designs of a leader,
To show us their way,
Sacred alignments,
In the lines of lay.

The profound nature,
Of the inner mind,
One who was created,
Out of new self design.

Essences Of Love

Your divine essence,
Connection to the source,
The truest of inspiration,
Its nature empowers,
My weary worn soul,
To once more aspire,
Then try to overcome,
The boundaries dividing,
Your profound inspiration,
Of such a pure soul,
Who still holds out,
For an energy of heart,
And will of the soul,
For the sacred essences,
And the uniqueness,
Of truest purest love.

Dare I Ask Her?

Will she lift my spirit,
To a higher ground,
And inspire my world,
With a dream so profound.

Will she show me the essences,
Of the reality of our love,
Creating an Earth down below,
Of the heavens perfection above.

Will she inspire inside a feeling,
Of truest and purest joy,
Will she ask to be my girl,
If I offer to be her boy.

Will we share a unifying harmony,
Felt for each other in our hearts,
The essences of our natures,
In the dynamics of our arts.

Will she create for me a place,
In the subtlety of her soul,
In love completely connected,
My half lived life turned whole.

Loving Obsession

This romantic infatuation,
Is driving me insane,
Thoughts of you in my mind,
Over & over and again & again.

The subtle addiction to your magic,
Stirring the elements of my will,
For every time I think of you,
I feel a buzz, a rush and a thrill.

I imaginer you are with me,
Bodies laying side by side,
Connecting energies of our spirits,
Through spiritualised empathic minds.

The energies of my heart and will,
Manifesting in this my obsession,
Do we still share the warmth of love,
Through our souls divine connection.

We need to talk for I have to know,
If deep down you feel the same,
Are we connected through harmony,
Or have I lost reason and gone insane.

Our Higher Nature

The essences,
Of our hearts,
Manifest,
In our will,
Reflects,
The complex dynamics,
Of our self,
And our higher nature,
Through looking,
Inside ourselves,
We can discover,
True control,
Over our emotions,
And the chaos,
Of the impulses,
And the desires,
That we experience,
In the dual manifestation,
Of the thoughts,
And the perceptions,
Of the intuitions,
The inner reality
Of the human will.

Empathic Bond

I feel the magic,
Of the love,
Between our souls,
The fire and energy,
So truly profound,
I feel its resonance,
Between our beings,
The sublime vibration,
Such a subtle dynamic
Manifest and pure,
Within the nature,
Of our beings,
And the nature,
Of the soul essence,
Within my heart,
For between its beats,
There is a space,
Reserved only for you,
And the inspiration,
The pure creativity,
And the enlightenment,
Which you bring,
To my soul.

Essences Of Perception

As we settle,
The inner chaos,
Of the innate,
Raw dispositions,
Of the emotional,
The instinctual,
The intellectual,
And the intuitive,
Nature of the will,
Manifesting from within,
Finding a space inside,
For isomorphic imagination,
For the representation,
Of the emotions,
And the thoughts,
Of other people,
Experiential perceptions,
Of higher intuition,
Created through cultivating,
A serene noble heart,
And tranquil inner nature,
Of the dynamics of emotion,
Channelling its emergence,
As the perception of our ideas.

<u>Dispositions Of The Will</u>

Feel the vibration,
Of the energy,
The empowerment,
Of your true self,
A pure flow,
Within the will,
Its invigorating nature,
And profound essence,
So manifests for us,
In the inner dynamics,
Of our beings,
Uplifted and inspired,
Through the unity,
Between the core,
Of the soul,
And the outermost edges,
Of spiritual perception,
Forming a nexus of unity,
Between mind and matter,
The unfiltered perceptions,
Pure intuitive representation,
Of the true nature of reality.

Flow Of Intuitions

All we know,
Of reality,
Is the intuition,
Of a transduced,
Mental representation,
Of the surface level,
Manifestation of form,
In our experiences,
Of the nature,
Of our realities,
For the knowledge,
Of the real depths,
And truer nature,
Of inner reality,
Is both a boundary,
And a frontier,
Of the endeavours,
Of human exploration,
And the limits,
Of being and mind,
Contained in the weave,
Of the subconscious,
Nature of perceptions.

Higher Learning

As the dynamics,
Of our perspective
Refine unto perfections,
Of the inspired soul,
Through the evolution,
Of the core self,
Into a dynamic,
Which represents,
The manifestation,
Of the essence,
Our hopes and ideals,
As the embodiment,
And the empowerment,
Of our higher nature,
As the manifest will,
And the raw emotion,
Of our basic instincts,
Tempered and crafted,
Into the source,
Of the realisation,
Of the inner potential,
Of our higher nature.

<u>New Meanings</u>

The divine essence,
Of our inspired connection,
Empowers my being,
To press onwards,
And pursue further,
The virtue of the heart,
The inspiration of the soul,
And the love,
Held in our ideals,
And our higher nature,
Which manifests,
As the feelings,
Which we share,
In the essence,
Of the totality,
Of our awakened beings,
Growing and evolving,
Our new meanings,
Achieved through synthesis,
And the alignments,
Of concepts, signs and symbols,
Which shall redefine,
The nature of the self,
For another generation,
In search of it own truth.

The World Aura

I ask of nature,
The essence,
Of her heart,
And the dynamics,
Of her passion,
So as that,
I can vibrate,
With the beauty,
Of her love,
And the energies,
Of her being,
Which she feels,
As the totality,
Of the macrocosm,
Thought form apex,
Of spiritual awareness,
Connecting all life,
Through a gossamer web,
Of interconnected infinitudes,
Of the mystic wonder,
Of the empowered soul,
And unity of our beings.

Essences Of Nature

As we consider,
That which lay,
Beneath the surface,
Of our reality,
I ask of nature,
For her to reveal,
The sublime beauty,
Of her truth,
And her perfections,
Which only the wise,
Will ever comprehend,
For reason alone,
Cannot equate reality,
Only the creativity,
Of our capacity,
For the manifestation,
Of abstract will,
Can take the pieces,
Of deconstructed perception,
And truly define,
The boundaries,
Of thought and reality,
The essences of nature.

Thought Realities

As we think,
We project our ideas,
Out into the universe,
Their shape and form,
Embedded in the essence,
Of their vibrations,
In the patterns,
Of our will,
And the emotional flow,
Of instinctual nature,
Its receptive perception,
Of thought manifest,
Within the spaces,
Of the silent mind,
So we harmonise,
With the subtlety,
Our our aura,
And sublime nature,
The inner reality,
Of mental representation,
And thought content,
The enlightened energies,
Of a higher nature,
Connecting all life.

The Old Times

I am glad to see,
You have not changed,
For all the time,
Since our last adventure,
Every time we meet,
You always remind me,
Of a part of myself,
I thought I had lost,
Or totally forgotten,
To the sands of time,
That you still remember,
From our youth,
The eternal energy,
Of aspiring young hearts,
So full of inspiration,
The freedom and the passion,
Of our hopes and dreams,
So as we reminisce,
About the old days,
We relive the essences,
And energies of the will,
Alive in the moment,
Once more there,
Through meanings still shared.

Lost To The Anguish

As she cried,
Tears of blood,
From self-inflicted wounds,
She scattered the ashes,
Of her fallen immortal love,
Their unique connection severed,
By a knife of self sacrifice,
The introspective murder,
Of theurgic love and inspiration,
In a savage moment erased,
Through the inescapable pain,
Of the fires of hell,
The only lonely place,
She could hide from the truth,
From the torment of knowing,
Of her souls fractured core,
Its bitter broken shards,
Resonating the woe and anguish,
Of a brutally torn mind,
So lost to the despair,
And the tragic loss,
Of a forgotten trauma,
And its imprint upon her heart,
For the rest of her days.

First Contact

As I sketch the mind,
Of an alien perspective,
I ask of this creature,
What is the essence,
Of your true nature,
What are the dynamics,
Of your complex being,
And the interstellar legacy,
Your culture of enlightenment,
Inspired empathic will,
Creative self energy,
And science of the mind,
But what is the empowerment,
Which you so seek,
What are the alignments,
Of the concepts and symbols,
Which forms the web,
Of your unique perspective,
And to what extent,
Do our representations,
Match and correlate,
To a shared understanding,
Between our two cultures.

Inner Self

As I gaze,
Into the purity,
Of the depths,
Of your sublime soul,
I glimpse the beauty,
Of your love,
And the grace,
Of your enlightened heart,
As you sense,
The essence and form,
Of my being,
My higher nature,
Of sacred dynamics,
Calls to you,
To be here,
With me as an energy,
Within this moment,
That together,
We might share,
The harmony,
Of a unity of being
And the inspiration,
Of our inner higher nature.

Our Lover

The sacred energy,
Of our love,
Is the greatest,
Empowerment,
Ive ever felt,
The essence,
Of your grace,
Is the purest,
Of perfections,
In the universe,
Every time,
Our spirits touch,
Our souls share,
The sweet embrace,
Of true love,
Our hearts,
Sharing the energy,
Of our affections,
And the beauty,
Of our immortal,
True desires,
So lay with me,
And resonate,
The vibrations,
Of our love.

Cosmic Bliss

I wrap my arms,
Around your waist,
Your slender form,
So graceful,
I squeeze your shoulders,
With my hands,
As we kiss,
And cuddle,
The moonlight,
Makes us glow,
A brilliant,
Hue of blue,
As our desire,
Ascends reality,
And our spirits,
Merge into one,
On a higher plain,
Of celestial love,
Your sweet embrace,
Carrying me skyward,
To the cosmic bliss,
Of our idyllic sweet love.

Rock The Scene

I would like to be your boy,
So do not treat me like a toy,
Playing the long game for your hand,
The finest female of the land.

Every daydream is of you,
Revitalising till brand new,
The purity of your love refined,
By heart, soul, spirit and mind.

The essence of your undying affection,
The soft sublime and loving perfection,
The flawless beauty of your face,
And aura of such infinite grace.

I see your energy grow with every day,
Knowing of all of the sacred ways,
We feel our emotions as subtle beings,
Born to rule the heavens and rock the scene.

Into The Abyss

Even if we have,
Our truest day,
And we realise,
Our loving dream,
Will the fairytale,
Actually last forever,
Or will we,
Lose sight,
Of our love,
And burn,
The bridges,
We so carefully,
Have built,
Over the years,
And the passion,
That we have,
Within our hearts,
Fade and wane,
Becoming dull,
And mundane,
And the energies,
Of our love,
Disappears from our souls,
Back into the abyss.

Dream Girl

I adore you my hun,
Every bit of you,
Your tender heart,
Phenomenal mind,
Indestructible spirit,
And warm loving soul.
Every part of your being,
Is a true perfection.
As our subtle bodies,
Lay next to each other
And at nighttime,
We talk for hours,
Am I your space man?
Are you my dream girl?
As I hold you close,
And feel your heartbeat,
I sigh with relief,
And truly content I smile,
For you complete me,
My essences unified,
Made whole through your love.

Open Skies

The ultimate rave,
At the crest of our wave,
Was the human race saved?
From the end of its days?

Now unstoppable and free,
Emancipated in positivity,
The true love and possibility,
Of our spiritual connectivity.

The deep subconscious mind,
To an infinity refined,
A self created new design,
To a plan so divine.

So my brethren do not hide,
Stand here by my side,
And let me be your guide,
As the skies open wide.

Connective Empowerment

The rush so unreal,
As in a crowd,
Our eyes first meet,
Connected together,
Through our essences,
As our hearts beat,
Our spirits soar high,
United together,
Enlightened forever,
Once more,
The resonance,
Between our souls,
The sacred vibrations,
Empowers us on,
To once more,
Strive for better,
For the Human Race,
So that all people,
Can enjoy the peace,
And the equality,
To realise their dreams,
And achieve their aspirations,
Following their inspirations.

Universal Love

Through our love,
I see the world,
A different way,
Each and every day.
A place so divine,
With the inner beauty,
Of a higher nature.
On these long,
Warm summer nights,
With the scent,
Of the flowers,
Invigorating my soul,
I think deeply of us,
You my perfect girl,
And I imagine you now,
Are here with me,
Laying in my arms,
For our love is infinite,
And like the forces of nature,
Is eternal like the universe.

All Over Your Face!

You are a being,
Of such utter perfection,
How I desire your love,
And your subtle affection.

Your essence is truly,
Of such a sublime grace,
And beauty is so written,
All over your pretty face.

If I can be your space-man,
You can be my dream girl,
And together we shall rule,
The heavens, stars and world.

I cannot wait until,
The next time that we meet,
For the passion that we feel,
Is so unmistakably unique.

Interstellar Lovers

I would like for you to know,
That I do think of you so,
For the fire in your heart,
A revolution so could start.

With a sacred inner flame,
I hear you say my name,
For the wonders of your soul,
Heals and unites me until whole.

Upon the warm currents of love,
We fly to the stratosphere above,
Sailing the cosmic starry skies,
So young at heart yet old and wise.

So as we return from our quest,
We lay our weary hearts at rest,
For to me you are like no other,
My eternal and inspired interstellar lover.

Lightning Source UK Ltd.
Milton Keynes UK
UKHW020258080223
416610UK00016B/2067

9 781471 724329